Pita's Birthday
Contents

Ready to Read

School Publications Branch
Department of Education Wellington 1985

No One Likes Skinny Hens

a fable retold by Rowena Buckingham
pictures by Peter Bromhead

Once upon a time,
there were five hens
in a hen house.
Three hens were fat,
and two hens were skinny.

The fat hens
made fun of the skinny hens.
"You are too skinny.
No one likes skinny hens,"
said the three fat ones.

One day,
the cook looked in the hen house.
"Three fat hens," he said.
"Good!
I will cook them for dinner."

Then the fat hens
wanted to be skinny.
But it was too late!
The cook put them in the pot.

The skinny hens
ran out of the hen house.
"We are glad no one likes us!"
they said.

Dandelion Clock

A poem for sharing
by Joyce Le Pine

I'll find a dandelion clock
And break it off with care.
To tell the time I'll count the blows
Until the stalk is bare.

One o'clock, two o'clock,
   three o'clock, four,
Five o'clock, six o'clock,
   seven o'clock, more,
Eight o'clock, nine o'clock,
   ten o'clock, there—
Dandelion parachutes
   everywhere.

Rima Rakiraki

a traditional rhyme adapted by Bea Yates
pictures by Sheryll Touvelle-Wright

Rima rakiraki went out one day,

Over the hills and far away.

Mama Rakiraki called,

"Quack, quack, quack!"

But only wha rakiraki came back.

Wha rakiraki went out one day,
Over the hills and far away
Mama Rakiraki called,
"Quack, quack, quack!"
But only toru rakiraki came back.

Toru rakiraki went out one day,
Over the hills and far away.
Mama Rakiraki called,
"Quack, quack, quack!"
But only rua rakiraki came back.

Rua rakiraki went out one day,
Over the hills and far away.
Mama Rakiraki called,
"Quack, quack, quack!"
But only tahi rakiraki came back.

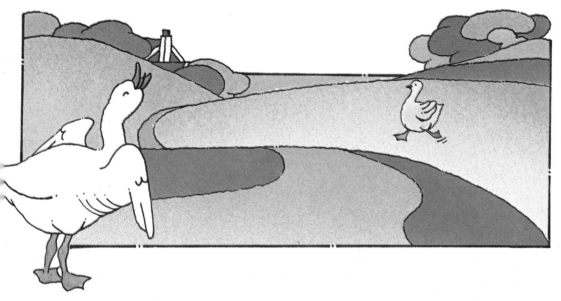

Tahi rakiraki went out one day,
Over the hills and far away.
Mama Rakiraki called,
"Quack, quack, quack!"
But no little rakiraki came back.

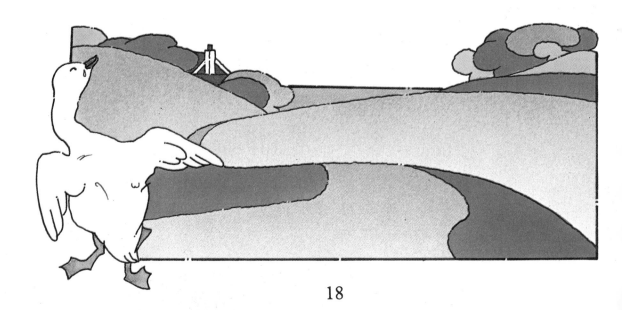

The Three Wise Men of Gotham

Three wise men of Gotham
Went to sea in a bowl;
If the bowl had been stronger,
My story would have been longer.

Anita Vink

A Proper Soccer Ball

by Glenda Laurence
pictures by Deirdre Gardiner

Rachel liked to play soccer.

At home, her big brother
played soccer with her.

But the boys at school
would not let her play soccer
with them.

Rachel's brother
got her a soccer ball
for her birthday.
It was a proper soccer ball,
with her name on.
Rachel took it to school.

Now the boys play soccer with her.

PITA'S BIRTHDAY

by Joy Cowley
pictures by
Murray Grimsdale

It was Pita's birthday.

His father cooked meat,
and taro,
and banana.
His mother cooked a cake.

Pita put on a record,
and all the family danced.
"You dance, Pita," they said.
Pita danced for the family.

His dog, Fasi, came in.
She ran up and down,
and barked.

"Hey!" said Pita.
"This isn't your birthday.
Out you go!"

Fasi's ears went down.
Her tail went down.

"Out! Out! Out!" said Pita.
So Fasi went out.

On the way,
she ate some of the cake.

Pita's Birthday Cards

Card 1 (top left):
x x x x x x x x x x x x x x x x x x x
Pita Kia ora
i to ra whano
arohanui Jonath

Card 2 (top right):
Manuia Iou Aso
Fanau

Card 3 (bottom left):
uia Manuia
Rava No toou
Ra Arauanga

Card 4 (bottom right):
Pita Manuia Iou A
Fanau Alofa atu
Happy birthday x x x x x

In Our Library...

by Sue Thurlow
pictures by Gavin Bishop

In our school, there's a library.
And in our library,
there's a library shelf.
And on the library shelf,
there's a library book.
And in the library book,
there's a library book pocket.
And in the library book pocket,
there's a library book card.
And behind that library book card—
there's a library book ghost.

Slowly, slowly,
the library book ghost floats
out from behind the library book card,
out of the library book pocket,
through the library book,
on to the library shelf,
and into the room.

"Reading is fun!" it whispers.

V. R. WARD, GOVERNMENT PRINTER, WELLINGTON, NEW ZEALAND—1985

32670C—85PT